First published in the United States, Great Britain, Canada, Australia, and New Zealand in 2010
by North-South Books Inc., an imprint of NordSüd Verlag AG, CH-8005 Zürich, Switzerland.
Distributed in the United States by North-South Books Inc., New York 10001.

Library of Congress Cataloging-in-Publication Data is available.
Printed in Belgium by Proost N.V., B 2300 Turnhout, April 2010.
ISBN: 978-0-7358-2323-5 (trade edition)
1 3 5 7 9 ♣ 10 8 6 4 2

www.northsouth.com

FSC
Mixed Sources
Product group from well-managed
forests and other controlled sources
Cert no. BV-COC-070303
www.fsc.org
© 1996 Forest Stewardship Council

Minako Chiba

The Somebody for Me

NorthSouth
New York / London

Miss Mika was a happy toy maker. "I hope all my dolls will be happy too," she said as she sewed.

"What is happy?" asked Sumiko.

Miss Mika smiled. "Happy is how you feel when somebody loves you."

The dolls sat in the toy shop window, waiting hopefully for somebody to love them.

"I want a little girl somebody," said one.

"I want a baby somebody," said another.

"I want a grandmother somebody," said a third. "Like Miss Mika."

"I just want the somebody for me," said Sumiko.

Many people came to the toy shop. The dolls were very popular. One by one, they all went home with somebody to love them.

But nobody chose Sumiko.

New toys came into the shop. And new
children came to choose those toys. Sumiko
watched them sadly.

"Where is the somebody for me?" she thought.

As the weeks passed, Sumiko got dustier and
dustier. Finally she was moved to a corner with
an old drum and a rolling wooden chicken.

"Nobody wants us," said the chicken.

But Sumiko felt sure the somebody for her
would come along one day.

Somebody came for the old drum, and somebody came for the rolling chicken, but still nobody came for Sumiko. "Where is the somebody for me?" she cried. With no one to love, she felt as if her heart was in prison.

And then one day a little girl came into the shop. She looked all around—until she saw Sumiko sitting alone in the corner. Sumiko's heart beat faster.

The little girl picked her up. "I want this one!" she said.

Sumiko could hardly believe her ears.

"That doll is old and dirty," said the girl's
father. "Let's find you something else. Something
new and clean."

Sumiko's heart sank.

Days passed. Sumiko could hardly bear her
sorrow. Could there really be no one for her?

❧

And then one day she heard somebody say,
"Do you still have that little doll? The one with
the striped legs and the long ears?"

It was the little girl! She picked up Sumiko and hugged her.

"Please, Daddy," the little girl said. "This is the one I love."

And this time her daddy said yes.

The little girl took Sumiko home and cleaned her up and hugged her and sang to her. And every night she tucked Sumiko tightly into bed, right next to her.

"Now I know what it feels like to be happy," thought Sumiko. "I have found the somebody for me."

The End